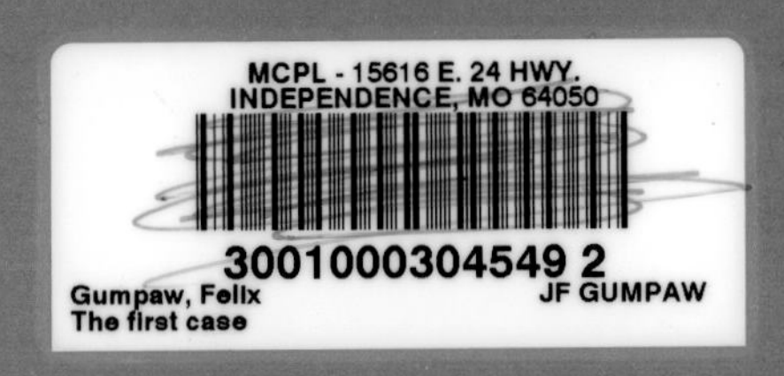

PUP
DETECT

VES

THE FIRST CASE

Written by FELIX GUMPAW
Illustrated by WALMIR ARCHANJO
at GLASS HOUSE GRAPHICS

LITTLE SIMON
NEW YORK LONDON TORONTO SYDNEY NEW DELHI

THIS BOOK IS A WORK OF FICTION. ANY REFERENCES TO HISTORICAL EVENTS, REAL PEOPLE, OR REAL PLACES ARE USED FICTITIOUSLY. OTHER NAMES, CHARACTERS, PLACES, AND EVENTS ARE PRODUCTS OF THE AUTHOR'S IMAGINATION, AND ANY RESEMBLANCE TO ACTUAL EVENTS OR PLACES OR PERSONS, LIVING OR DEAD, IS ENTIRELY COINCIDENTAL.

LITTLE SIMON
AN IMPRINT OF SIMON & SCHUSTER CHILDREN'S PUBLISHING DIVISION
1230 AVENUE OF THE AMERICAS, NEW YORK, NEW YORK 10020
FIRST LITTLE SIMON EDITION FEBRUARY 2021

ART AND COLOR BY WALMIR ARCHANJO, RAPHAEL KIRSCHNER, HUGO CARVALHO & JOÃO ZOD • COLORS BY WALMIR ARCHANJO & JOÃO ZOD • LETTERING BY MARCOS MASSAO INOUE • ART SERVICES BY GLASS HOUSE GRAPHICS • THE SIMON & SCHUSTER SPEAKERS BUREAU CAN BRING AUTHORS TO YOUR LIVE EVENT. FOR MORE INFORMATION OR TO BOOK AN EVENT CONTACT THE SIMON & SCHUSTER SPEAKERS BUREAU AT 1-866-248-3049 OR VISIT OUR WEBSITE AT WWW.SIMONSPEAKERS.COM.
DESIGNED BY NICHOLAS SCIACCA
MANUFACTURED IN CHINA 1120 SCP
10 9 8 7 6 5 4 3 2 1
LIBRARY OF CONGRESS CATALOGING-IN-PUBLICATION DATA
NAMES: GUMPAW, FELIX, AUTHOR. I GLASS HOUSE GRAPHICS, ILLUSTRATOR.
TITLE: THE FIRST CASE / BY FELIX GUMPAW ; ILLUSTRATED BY GLASS HOUSE GRAPHICS.
DESCRIPTION: FIRST LITTLE SIMON PAPERBACK EDITION. I NEW YORK : LITTLE SIMON, 2021. I SERIES: PUP DETECTIVES ; BOOK 1 I AUDIENCE: AGES 5-9 I AUDIENCE: GRADES 2-3 I SUMMARY: RIDER WOOFSON AND THE OTHER PUPPY DETECTIVES AT SCHOOL SET OUT TO NAB A CAFETERIA BANDIT. IDENTIFIERS: LCCN 2020024868 (PRINT) I LCCN 2020024869 (EBOOK) I ISBN 9781534474949 (PAPERBACK) I ISBN 9781534474956 (HARDCOVER) I ISBN 9781534474963 (EBOOK) SUBJECTS: LCSH: GRAPHIC NOVELS. I CYAC: GRAPHIC NOVELS. I MYSTERY AND DETECTIVE STORIES. I DOGS—FICTION. CLASSIFICATION: LCC PZ7.7.G858 FI 2021 (PRINT) I LCC PZ7.7.G858 (EBOOK) I DDC 741.5/973—DC23
LC RECORD AVAILABLE AT HTTPS://LCCN.LOC.GOV/2020024868
LC EBOOK RECORD AVAILABLE AT HTTPS://LCCN.LOC.GOV/2020024869

CONTENTS

CHAPTER 1
THIS IS PAWSTON ELEMENTARY SCHOOL.

SCHOOL
ZONE
PAWSTON
ELEMENTERY
SCHOOL

EVERY DAY, HUNDREDS OF STUDENTS WALK THROUGH THESE HALLWAYS.

MOST OF THEM BEHAVE LIKE GOOD STUDENTS SHOULD.

BUT PAWSTON ELEMENTARY SCHOOL ALSO HAS A DARKER SIDE.

THAT'S WHERE I COME IN.
SIMOON
I'M RIDER WOOFSON...
...THE GREATEST PUPPY DETECTIVE IN THE WHOLE SCHOOL.
PRIVATE
AND I JUST SPOTTED MY FIRST CLUE.

PRIVATE
PENCIL SHAVINGS!
2

RIDER, WHY AREN'T YOU IN CLASS?

I'M ON A CASE, MR. QUICK.

HERE'S MY HALL PASS.

PAWSTON
ELEMENTERY
SCHOOL
This hall pass is for RiderWoofson as he searches for missing pencils.
—Mrs. Plus, math teacher

HMM, WE'RE MISSING PENCILS IN OUR CLASS, TOO.

WITHOUT PENCILS, THE KIDS CAN'T TAKE TESTS.

I HOPE YOU FIND THEM!
PRIVATE
DON'T WORRY.
I WILL.

BUT MAYBE DON'T TELL EVERYONE THEY WILL HAVE TO TAKE TESTS BECAUSE OF ME.

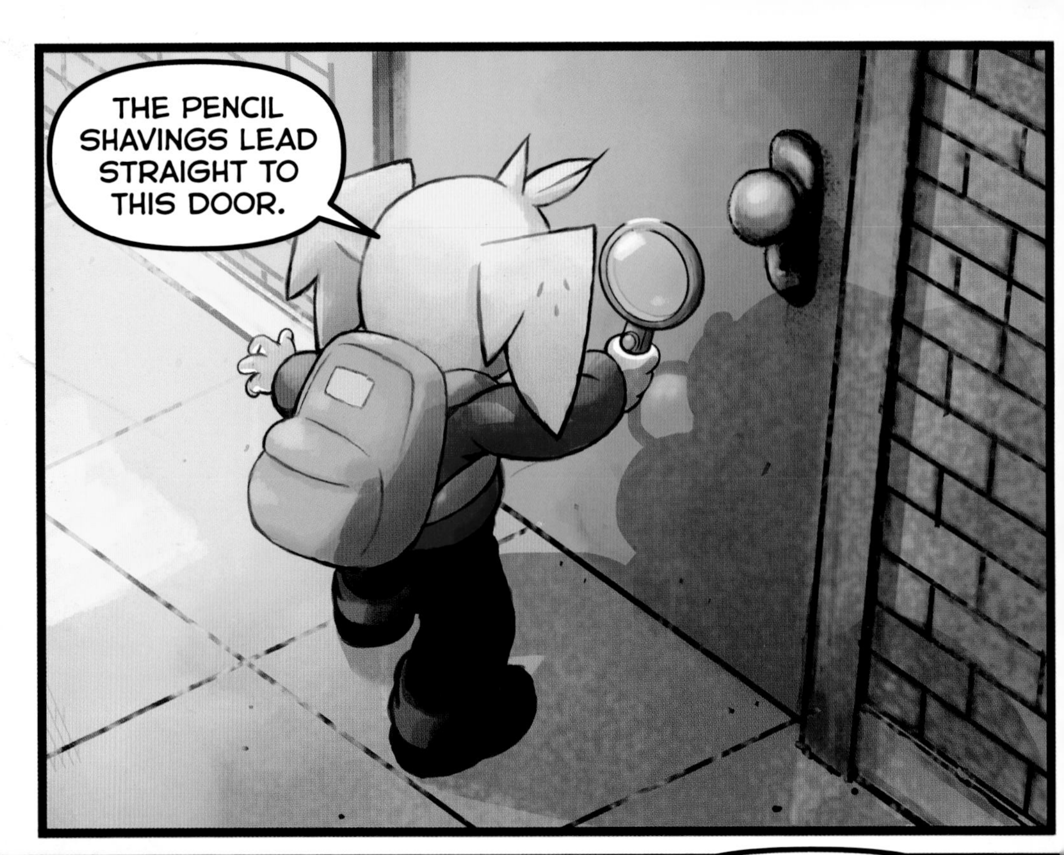
THE PENCIL SHAVINGS LEAD STRAIGHT TO THIS DOOR.

DON'T BOTHER. IT'S LOCKED.

YIKES!

VATE
WHO ARE YOU? AND WHY DID YOU SNEAK UP ON ME LIKE THAT?

I'M RORA GOODDOG. I WASN'T SNEAKING UP ON YOU!
I'M WORKING ON A CASE!
A CASE?

SOME STUDENTS ARE MISSING THEIR ERASERS!
I FOLLOWED A TRAIL OF PENCIL SHAVINGS TO THIS DOOR.

BECAUSE WHERE THERE'S A PENCIL, THERE'S ALWAYS AN ERASER!

HMM, I'M LOOKING FOR MISSING PENCILS.
I FOLLOWED THE PENCIL SHAVINGS TOO.

MAYBE WE SHOULD TEAM UP?
WELL, TWO HEADS ARE BETTER THAN ONE.
LET'S GO!

PRIVATE

PRIVATE
THWACK!

PRIVATE
WATCH OUT!
I'M GOING TO HAVE TO BREAK THE DOOR DOWN!

OR WE COULD JUST USE THE KEY.

PRIVATE
WHERE DID YOU GET THOSE?!

I BORROWED THEM FROM THE PRINCIPAL.

THE TEACHERS DON'T LIKE GRADING TESTS WITH WRONG ANSWERS SCRATCHED OUT INSTEAD OF ERASED.
SO THE PRINCIPAL TOLD ME I COULD USE ANYTHING I NEEDED.

PRIVATE
ANYTHING?
ANYTHING.
NOW LET'S SEE WHAT'S BEHIND THIS LOCKED DOOR.

BROKEN
PENCILS ARE
POINTLESS!

IT'S PENCIL-CRACKING TIME!
THESE PENCIL FIGHTS ARE KIND OF SKETCHY.
I THOUGHT TURTLES HAD HARD SHELLS!
WELCOME TO PENCIL-PAIN-YA!

WHAT A TERRIBLE WASTE OF SCHOOL SUPPLIES.
LOOKS LIKE WE FOUND A SECRET PENCIL-FIGHTING CLUB.

THWACK!

I WIN! YOU LOSE!
GIVE ME YOUR ERASER, DUDE!

WE'VE GOT TO STOP THIS!
WAIT!

LET'S GET THE PRINCIPAL.
WE SOLVED THE MYSTERY.
PRIVATE
HE CAN TAKE IT FROM HERE.

NO FLY

THANKS, RIDER AND RORA.
YOU TWO DETECTIVES MAKE A PRETTY GOOD TEAM.

A TEAM, HUH? WHAT DO YOU THINK, RORA?
I THINK WE NEED TO FIND A NEW MYSTERY.

CHAPTER 2
LITTLE DID WE KNOW...

THINGS SEEM QUIET.
MILK
MILK

YEAH...

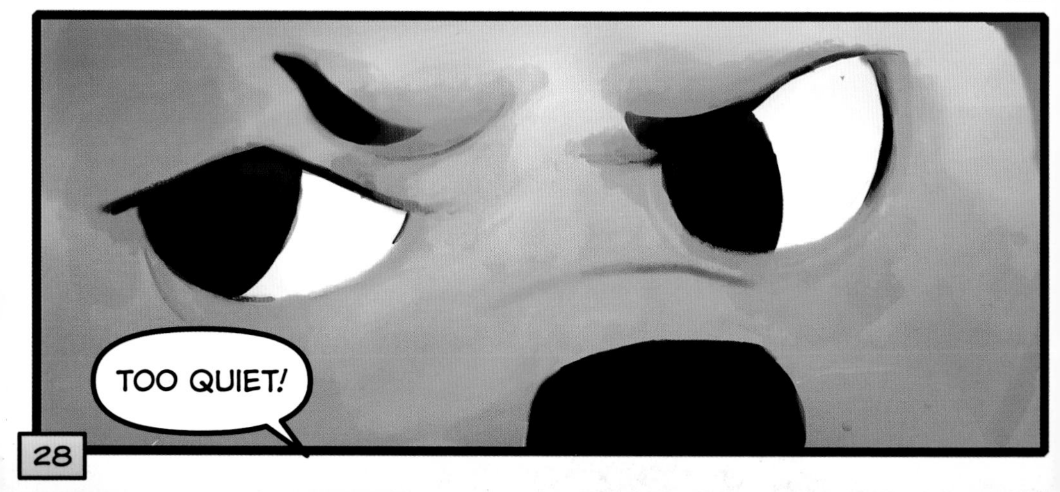
TOO QUIET!

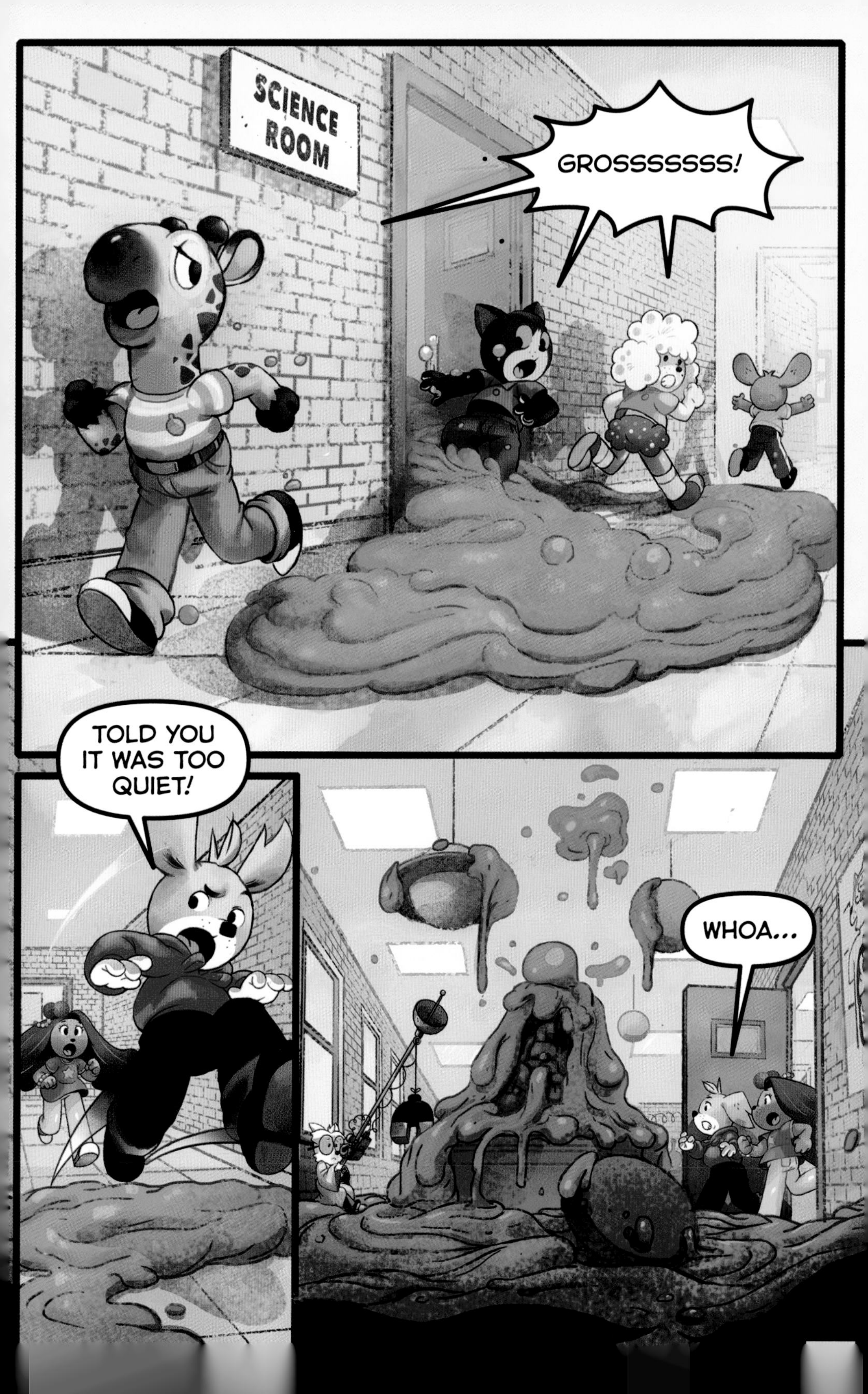
SCIENCE ROOM
GROSSSSSSS!
TOLD YOU IT WAS TOO QUIET!
WHOA...

LOOK!
IT'S OUR FIRST SUPER-VILLAIN!
LET'S STOP HIM!
FREEZE, DR. SLIME!
YEAH!
NO MORE MESS FROM YOU, MR. MESS!
MR. MESS?
I KIND OF LIKED DR. SLIME...

WHO'S DR. SLIME? OR MR. MESS?
I'M WESTIE BARKER!

I'M TRYING TO STOP THE SLIME WITH MY SUPER SOAKER-UPPER!

NOW LET ME GET YOU OUT OF THIS STICKY SITUATION!

OKAY! BUT NO FUNNY BUSINESS!

SLIMY
SLIME SORD
IT WORKED!

YEAH IT DID!
BUT IF THERE IS NO SUPER-VILLAIN...
THEN WHO BUILT THE SLIME VOLCANO?

WELL, IT WAS...
...ME?

YOU SEE, I'M AN INVENTOR...
A&Z
SCIENCE

...AND I BUILT THIS VOLCANO!

EXCEPT IT GOT A LITTLE OUT OF CONTROL.

MORE LIKE A *LOT* OUT OF CONTROL!

HEY, IT WAS A MISTAKE, RIGHT?
AT LEAST THE SUPER SOAKER-UPPER WORKED.

DEFINITELY A MISTAKE.
INVENTIONS CAN BE...
UNPREDICTABLE.
HMM, SAY...

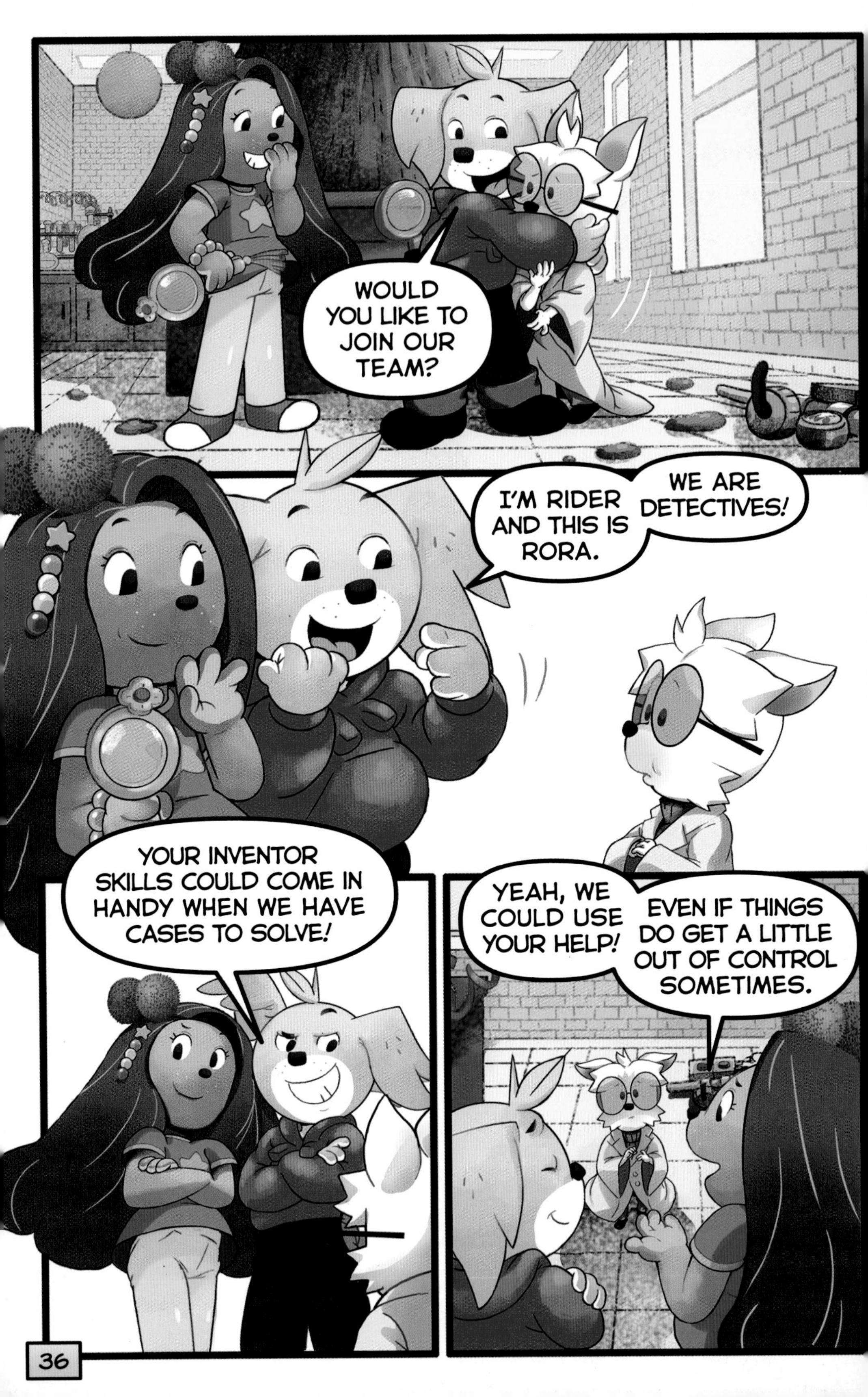
WOULD YOU LIKE TO JOIN OUR TEAM?
I'M RIDER AND THIS IS RORA.
WE ARE DETECTIVES!
YOUR INVENTOR SKILLS COULD COME IN HANDY WHEN WE HAVE CASES TO SOLVE!
YEAH, WE COULD USE YOUR HELP!
EVEN IF THINGS DO GET A LITTLE OUT OF CONTROL SOMETIMES.

= YeS!!!
COUNT ME IN!

CHAPTER 3
OUR FIRST MYSTERY IS OUR BIGGEST YET.
FINDING OUT WHAT'S IN THE SOUP OF THE DAY!
IT SMELLS LIKE YOUR VOLCANO SLIME, WESTIE!
BLECH! THIS SMELLS WAY WORSE!

BOW-WOWZA! NOW I SMELL LIKE VOLCANO SLIME!
TODAY SPECIAL:
SURPRISE SOUP

SORRY!
WOW. THAT IS ONE ANGRY LUNCH LADY!

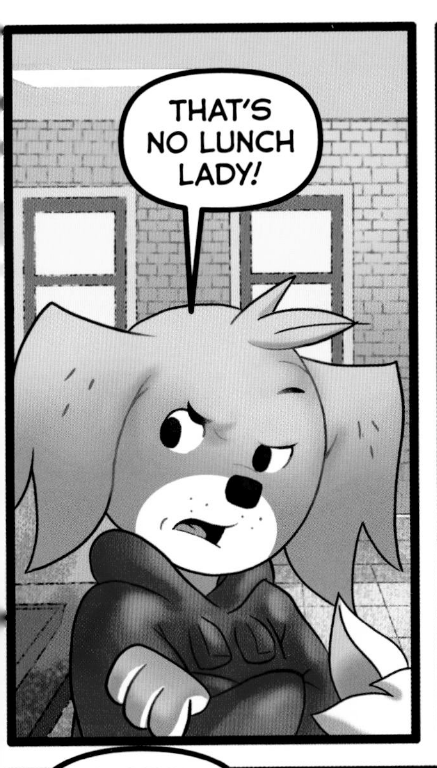
THAT'S NO LUNCH LADY!

DID YOU SEE THE WAY SHE LICKED THE SOUP OFF HER ARM?

A *REAL* LUNCH LADY WOULD KNOW NOT TO EAT THE SOUP.

HE'S RIGHT.
THAT'S CALLED THINKING LIKE A DETECTIVE!

TODAY
Elementary

HEY! STOP, THIEF!
NAB THOSE NOODLE NABBERS!
WE WILL STOP THOSE SPAGHETTI STEALERS!
THOSE RIGATONI ROBBERS!
UM... FARFALLE FIENDS!

WHATEVER THEY ARE CALLED, WE NEED TO GET THEM!
UH-OH! WE'VE GOT A PASTA PROBLEM!
I STILL LIKE "SPAGHETTI STEALERS" THE BEST!
WELL, THIS IS A MESSY MYSTERY!

I KNOW HOW TO PUT AN END TO THIS MEATBALL MAYHEM!

TRY TO FOCUS ON CATCHING THE BAD GUYS, WESTIE!
SORRY... MY BAD!
THIS IS MY FETCH-A-CHINI NOODLE!
GOTCHA!

YOUR DAYS OF MEALTIME MADNESS ARE OVER!
BOW-WOWZA! I'M NOT A THIEF!
I'M THE GOOD GUY!

THEN WHY ARE YOU WEARING A DISGUISE?

BECAUSE I'M UNDERCOVER!
YOU NEED A GOOD COSTUME TO CATCH BAD GUYS IN THE ACT!

YOU MIGHT WANT TO LOOK UP THE WORD "GOOD."

WE CAUGHT YOU RED-HANDED!
OH, THIS? IT'S PASTA SAUCE!

HI. I'M ZIGGY FLUFFENSTUFF!
I'VE BEEN AFTER THE LUNCHTIME BANDIT FOR WEEKS!
AND THANKS TO YOU, HE'S GONE AND I'M STARVING!
WHAT AM I GOING TO EAT NOW THAT THOSE YUMMY MEATBALLS ARE GONE?

SOUP SURPRISE?
YUCK! NO WAY!

SO WHO ARE YOU THREE, ANYWAY?

WE'RE THE ONES WHO WILL HELP YOU CATCH THE LUNCHTIME BANDIT!

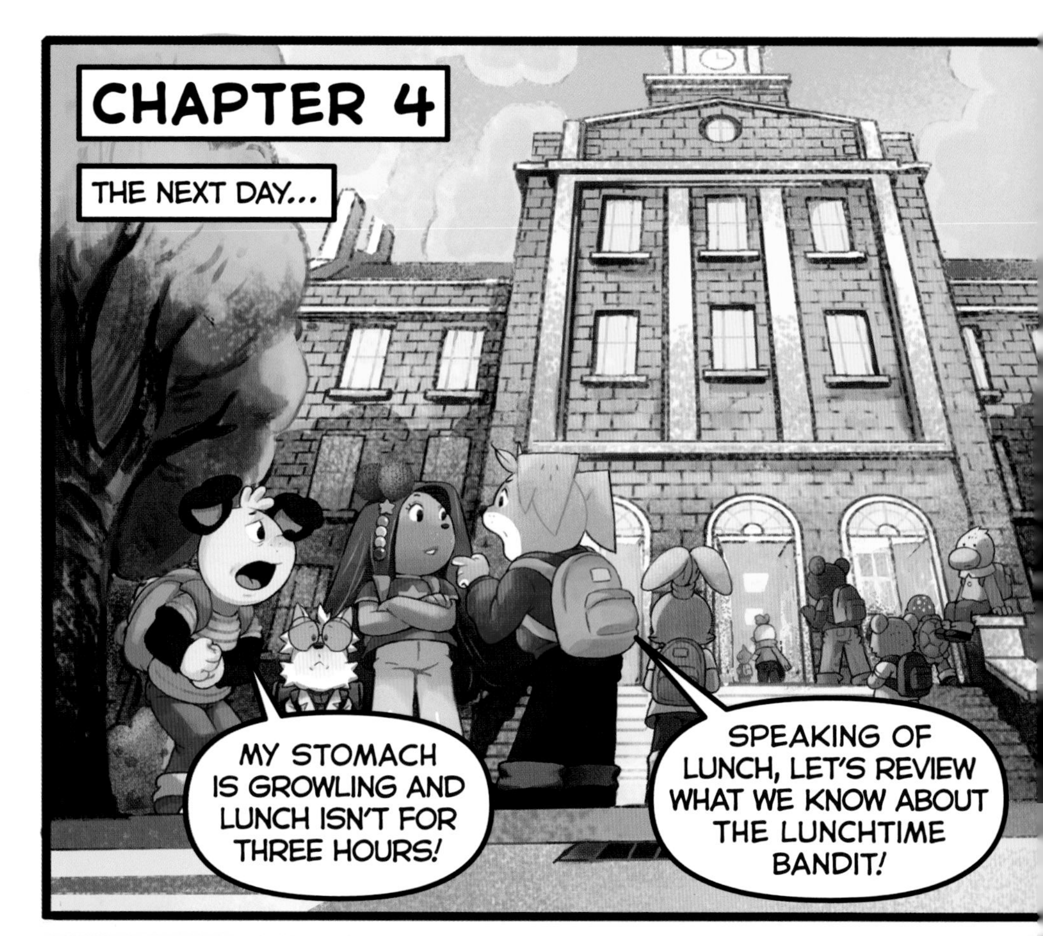

CHAPTER 4
THE NEXT DAY...
MY STOMACH IS GROWLING AND LUNCH ISN'T FOR THREE HOURS!
SPEAKING OF LUNCH, LET'S REVIEW WHAT WE KNOW ABOUT THE LUNCHTIME BANDIT!

HE STRIKES AT LUNCHTIME!

HE MUST LOVE TO EAT!
I ASKED AROUND, AND HE IS NOT ONE OF THE CAFETERIA COOKS.

NO, HE'S A CAFETERIA CROOK!
GOOD ONE!
OKAY, SO WE DON'T KNOW MUCH YET.
BUT WE DO KNOW ONE THING...
WE NEED TO STOP HIM BEFORE HE STRIKES AGAIN!

TODAY'S SPEIAL:
BEAN
BURRITOS
I HOPE SO.
TODAY'S LUNCH IS MY FAVORITE...
BEAN BURRITOS!
WHAT WE NEED IS A *PLAN!*

OOOH, I HAVE AN IDEA!
Eel = P.Δt

LET'S REPLACE THE GOOD BEANS WITH STINKY ONES!

WHY WOULD WE DO THAT TO THE POOR, DELICIOUS BEANS?
SO THE BANDIT WILL STEAL THE STINKY BEANS...
AND WE CAN FOLLOW THE STINK TO WHEREVER HE IS HIDING!
LET'S MAKE THIS THIEF A HAS-*BEAN*!

GREAT JOB GETTING THE CAFETERIA LADIES TO USE THE STINKY BEANS!
THEY WANT TO NAB THIS THIEF AS MUCH AS WE DO!
NOT SO FAST, BANDIT!
DROP THE BEANS AND PUT YOUR PAWS UP!

WHATEVER YOU SAY!
HOW ABOUT YOU, ROTTEN?
ANY CHANCE YOU KNOW THE ANSWER?
2014
I CAN'T BELIEVE I KNOW THE ANSWER FOR ONCE!
I CAN'T WAIT TO SHOW EVERYONE...

...HOW SMART I REALLY AM...
WHAAAA?

EWWW.
THOSE BEANS STINK!
ROTTEN LUCK, KID!
HEY! THOSE BEANS STINK!
LIKE YOU STINK AT MATH!

THE BANDIT TOSSED OUR TRAP ON THAT POOR PUP!
MAN, THAT STINKS!
I FEEL BAD FOR HIM!
SHOULD WE STOP AND HELP HIM?
THE TEACHER WILL HELP HIM!
THE BEST THING WE CAN DO IS CATCH THE BANDIT!

HE'S TOO FAST!
WHO KNEW KOALAS COULD RUN LIKE THAT?
WE CAN'T CATCH HIM.

LET'S GO BACK TO THE SCENE OF THE CRIME AND LOOK FOR CLUES!

CHAPTER 5

MENU

TO SOLVE THIS CASE, WE NEED TO THINK LIKE CRIMINALS!

ZIGGY, HOW WERE YOU ABLE TO SNEAK IN YESTERDAY?
I WORE A DISGUISE, REMEMBER?

THAT'S IT! THE BANDIT USES DISGUISES!
I'VE SEEN SOME MYSTERIOUS ANIMALS AROUND HERE...

LIKE YESTERDAY, WHEN HE WAS A LUNCH LADY...
MILK
AND BEFORE THAT, THERE WAS A MILKMAN I'D NEVER SEEN BEFORE...
ONE TIME HE WAS A BAKER...
AND ONE DAY...
A PICKLE DELIVERY ELEPHANT.
SOME DISGUISES MAKE MORE SENSE THAN OTHERS.

GREAT THINKING!
SO NOW WE KNOW HE LIKES DISGUISES.
WE JUST NEED TO KNOW HOW HE SNEAKS IN!
EXIT
MAYBE HE CAME IN THROUGH THE SKYLIGHT!
THAT'S RIGHT!
BAD GUYS LOVE SKYLIGHTS!
THEY REALLY DO!
NO DICE! I CHECKED.
IT'S LOCKED!

WHAT IF...
HE USED AN ARMY OF MICRO-BOTS?
THEY COULD SNEAK INSIDE AND STEAL ALL THE FOOD!

OR AT LEAST THAT'S WHAT I WOULD DO!
NICE DAYDREAM.
BUT WE SAW HIM STEAL THE FOOD, REMEMBER?
DRAT! YOU'RE RIGHT!
YOU KNOW WHAT? I SHOULD INVENT THEM!
MAYBE AFTER WE'VE SOLVED THE CASE, WESTIE!

HEY, MISS LUNCH LADY!
MENU
SOUP SURPRISE
DANGER: too MANY BaNaNaS

BANANAS!
WHAT'S WITH ALL THE BANANAS?

MENU
SOUP SURPRISE
meatloaf and bread
(no bananas!)
DANGER: TOO MANY BANANAS!
I DON'T SEE ANYTHING ABOUT BANANA PUDDING? AND ALSO...
...CAN I HAVE A BANANA?

NO IDEA!
WE DIDN'T ORDER THEM.
MENU
Banana pudding, banana cake and banana ...
SO IT LOOKS LIKE WE ARE HAVING A BANANA MENU TOMORROW!
MENU
THIS HAS TO BE THE WORK OF THE BANDIT!
CAN I STILL HAVE ONE?
THE BANDIT MUST LOVE BANANAS!
HE WANTS YOU TO COOK SOME BANANA TREATS FOR HIM TO STEAL!

I REFUSE TO COOK FOR THAT THIEF!
WOULD YOU IF IT COULD HELP CATCH THE BANDIT?
DANGER: TOO MANY BANANAS
I HAVE A PLAN.
IT MIGHT BE BANANAS...
MENU
SOUP SURPRISE
meatloaf and bread
(no bananas!)
...BUT BANANAS ENOUGH TO WORK!
UM... I'M PRETTY HUNGRY.
CAN I HAVE THAT BANANA OR NOT?

ONLY AT THE CAFETERIA!
SPECIAL MENU!
BANANA SPECIAL MENU!
LARGEST BANANA SPLIT IN THE WORLD!
ONE DAY ONLY AT THE CAFETERIA!
THIS SHOULD GET THE BANDIT'S ATTENTION!
GOOD WORK, WESTIE! NOW, EVERYONE...
...KEEP YOUR EYES PEELED!
ONE DA
ONLY
AT THE

ONE DAY ONLY
SPECIAL
GET IT? LIKE BANANA PEELS?
LET'S BE SERIOUS, RORA...
...BUT GOOD ONE!
REMEMBER, EVERYONE.... WE CAN'T AFFORD TO SLIP UP.

GET IT? SLIP UP?
LIKE ON A BANANA PEEL?

HEY GANG.
LOOK AT MY COOL COSTUME!
ONE DAY ONLY AT THE CAFETERIA!
EVERY STUDENT GOT ONE TO CELEBRATE THE GIANT BANANA SPLIT!

SPECIAL
LARGEST

CHAPTER 6
IT'S BANANA FEVER!
AT THE CAFETERIA!
LARGES BANANA DIVISION IN THE WORLD!
LARGES BANANA DIVISION IN THE WORLD!
LARGES BANANA DIVISION IN THE WORLD!

THE LUNCHTIME BANDIT IS ONTO US.
HE MUST BE THE ONE WHO GAVE EVERYONE THE COSTUMES.
I THINK YOU'RE RIGHT...

IT'S A BUNCH OF BANANAS!
ONE OF THEM *MUST* BE THE BANDIT!
BUT WHICH ONE?
LOOK FOR ANYTHING OUT OF THE ORDINARY!
IN A ROOM FULL OF GIANT BANANAS?
OVER THERE!

WE KNOW THE BANDIT IS TALL...
JUST LIKE THAT BANANA!

GREAT WORK, PUP DETECTIVES!

TIME TO PLAY FETCH!

HEY!
THAT'S SUPPOSED TO BE FOR EVERYONE TO SHARE!
HAVE A BANANA ON ME!

HE'S SLIPPING AWAY!
SO ARE WE!

FINALLY... A BANANA FOR ME!

ZIGGY, THAT WAS NOT A REAL BANANA.
CLOSE ENOUGH!
EXCUSE ME!
I NEED TO BORROW A FEW OF THOSE!

HEY, YOU'RE NOT HITTING HIM!

ALSO... YOU'RE WASTING YUMMY PIES!

I'M MISSING ON PURPOSE!

IT WILL FORCE THE BANDIT INTO THE GYM!

GREAT THINKING, RORA!
THE FRONT DOOR IS THE ONLY WAY IN OR OUT OF THE GYM!
WE'VE GOT YOU NOW, BANDIT!

GET READY TO DO TIME!
FOR SKIPPING THE LUNCH LINE!

WE KNEW YOU WOULD NAB THE BANANA SPLIT!
SO WE TURNED IT INTO A BANANA SPLAT!

YOU'RE GOING TO GO **BANANAS** OVER MY NEW INVENTION!

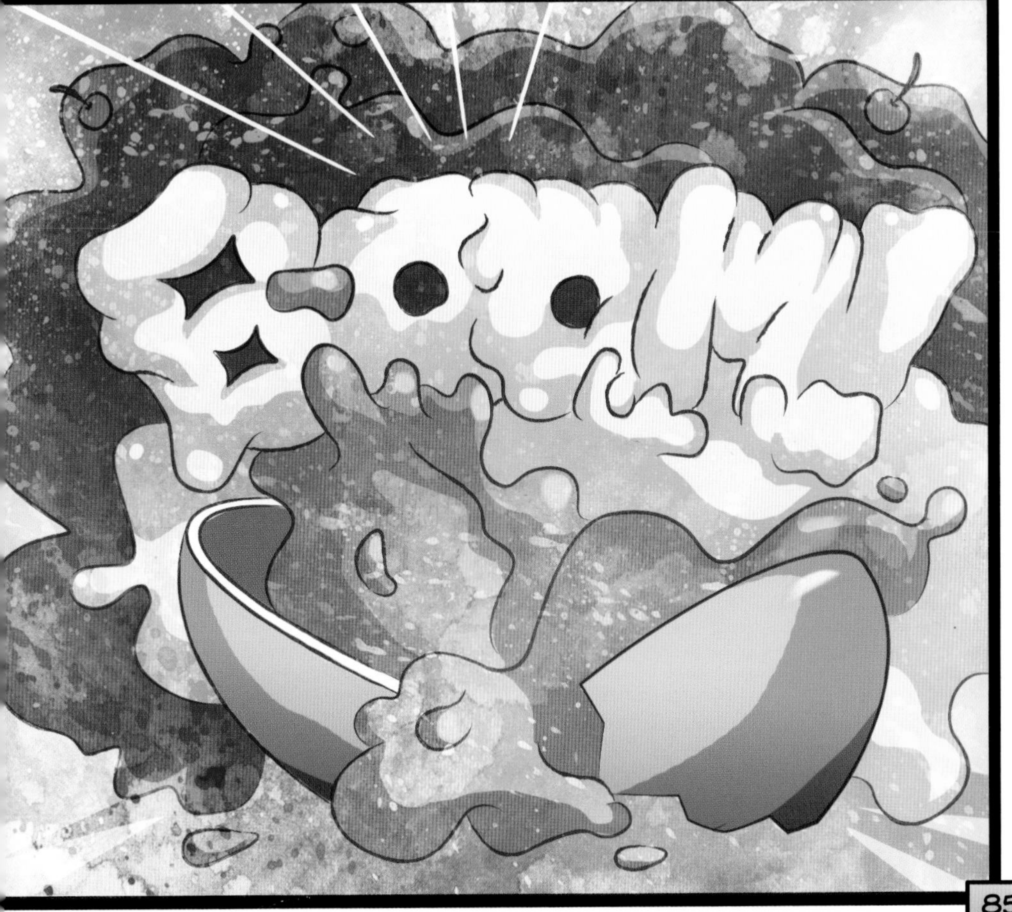

CHAPTER 7

HE ESCAPED!

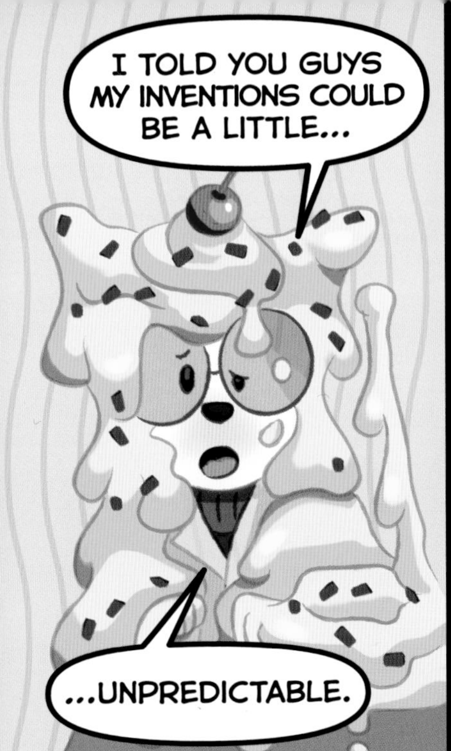
I TOLD YOU GUYS MY INVENTIONS COULD BE A LITTLE...
...UNPREDICTABLE.

AND I TOLD YOU BAD GUYS LOVE SKYLIGHTS!

MMMM... NEEDS MORE FUDGE SAUCE!

I ♥ BREAKING PENCILS
THE LUNCHTIME BANDIT STRIKES AGAIN!

LOOK!
WHAT IS THIS?
WAIT...
WHO IS THAT?

ZIGGY? WHAT'S UP?
I SMELL... WHIPPED CREAM...
...AND... BANANAS?

THAT KOALA WAS NO KOALA AT ALL!
HE DUPED US WITH A DOUBLE DISGUISE!
THAT BUNNY IS OUR BANDIT!

LET'S GO, RUFFHOUSE!

R

FASTER!
HOP TO IT!
FASTER, ROTTEN!
WE'VE ALMOST LOST THEM!

THOSE GOODY-GOODY PUP DETECTIVES...
...THOUGHT THEY COULD STOP ME!
THEY DON'T REALIZE HOW FUN IT IS...

...TO BE BAD!

THAT'S WHY I'M HELPING YOU...
...'CAUSE I'M A REAL BAD PUP!
THAT'S WHY THEY CALL ME...

ROTTEN
RUFFHOUSE

YEAH, I KNOW WHO YOU ARE!
THAT'S WHY I ASKED YOU TO HELP ME!
I'M JUST HAPPY TO GET BACK AT THEM!
THOSE LOUSY LUNCHTIME BANDITS, MESSING EVERYTHING UP FOR ME THE ONE TIME I KNEW THE ANSWER IN MATH CLASS!

WH–WHAT? THEY AREN'T THE BANDITS!
YES THEY ARE! AREN'T THEY?
IT WAS THEM AND THEIR KOALA FRIEND!
RIGHT?

THE KOALA?
YOU FOOL!
THAT KOALA WAS ME!
WHAAAAAAAA! I'M SO CONFUSED!

THAT WAS JUST A DISGUISE!
I'M THE LUNCHTIME BANDIT!
JUST ME!
THOSE PUPS WERE TRYING TO STOP ME!
BUT I WAS TOO CLEVER!
I HAVE SO MANY DISGUISES!
DISGUISES
I ♥ BREAKING PENCILS
AND I STOLE SO MANY LUNCHES!

NO ONE EVER SNIFFED ME OUT!
I ♥ BREAKING PENCILS
BUT...BUT... WHY?
BECAUSE I WAS HUNGRY !!!!!

THOSE GREEDY LUNCH LADIES!
THEY NEVER GAVE ME ENOUGH TO EAT!
EVEN WHEN I ASKED FOR SECONDS!
THEY ALWAYS SAID NO!
SO I BECAME...

CHAPTER 8
THE LUNCHTIME BANDIT!
I ♥ BREAKING PENCILS

AND I STOLE IT ALL!
BURGERS, TACOS!
MACARONI AND CHEESE!
AND MY FAVORITE...
...BANANAS!

I STOLE IT ALL SO EVERYONE WOULD FEEL AS HUNGRY AS ME!
NOW THAT YOU KNOW THE SCOOP...
...YOU'D BETTER NOT SPILL THE BEANS!!!

WAIT!
YOU ARE THE
BANDIT?

AND YOU DON'T WANT ME TO *SPILL THE BEANS?*

SPILL THE BEANS?

IT WAS YOU!
BREAKING PENCILS

YOU SPILLED THOSE BEANS ON ME!

WHAT'S THE BIG DEAL?
SO YOU GOT A LITTLE MESSY?
I GOT YOU OUT OF MATH CLASS, RIGHT?

WOW!
YOU'RE REALLY MAD ABOUT THOSE BEANS!
I ♥ BREAKING PENCILS
NO OFFENSE, BUT YOU REALLY STINK AT MATH!
YOU SHOULD BE GLAD I GOT YOU OUT OF–

GRRRRRRR!
HEY!
WHERE ARE YOU GOING?

I'M GOING TO TRY TO MAKE THIS RIGHT!

MEANWHILE...
I DON'T THINK WE CAN CATCH THEM.
GOOD TRY, EVERYONE. WE ALMOST-
WAIT! IS THAT THEM?

ARE THEY
COMING RIGHT
TOWARD US?

CHAPTER 9

THIS ISN'T THE WAY TO MY SECRET TREE HOUSE!
COME ON, THIS ISN'T FUNNY!

YOU'RE THE GETAWAY DRIVER.
YOU'RE SUPPOSED TO GET US AWAY!
NOT DRIVE BACK TO THE SCENE OF THE CRIME!
THIS WASN'T PART OF THE PLAN!

OH, DIDN'T I TELL YOU?
CHANGE OF PLANS!

LOOK! THAT DOG IS ON THE LOOSE!
HE ISN'T SLOWING DOWN!
WATCH OUT!

HEY, LUNCHTIME BANDIT!
NOW IT'S MY TURN...
...TO SPILL THE BEANS!

EXIT
CAFETERIA DUMPSTER

UGGH!
IT SMELLS ROTTEN!
WHAT'S THE BIG DEAL?
IT'S JUST A LITTLE MESSY, RIGHT?
ALSO I DON'T STINK AT MATH!

BOW-WOWZA!
HE FELL RIGHT INTO THE ROTTEN BEANS!
I THINK I FINALLY LOST MY APPETITE.

HELP ME! PLEASE!
THESE BEANS ARE SO... SLIPPERY!
WHY SHOULD WE HELP YOU?
ESPECIALLY AFTER ALL THE TROUBLE YOU CAUSED!
I'LL NEVER STEAL LUNCHES AGAIN. I SWEAR!

LOOKS LIKE WE GOT OUR CONFESSION!

WESTIE?
ON IT, RIDER!

CHAPTER 10
I KNEW THIS WOULD COME IN HANDY AGAIN!

WOW, THAT IS A GROSS TON OF GROSS!
HEY, I KNOW YOU FROM MY MATH CLASS!

YOU MIGHT BE GOOD AT DISGUISES, BUT YOU'RE PRETTY LOUSY AT MATH!

SO WHAT IF I STINK AT MATH?
WHY DOES EVERYONE CARE SO MUCH ABOUT THAT?

JUST, PLEASE!
GET THIS STINKY BEAN JUICE OFF ME!

WELL, WE JUST SOLVE CRIMES!
THAT'S RIGHT!
AND IT'S TIME FOR YOU TO OWN UP TO WHAT YOU DID!
SPEAKING OF WHICH...

...HERE COMES PRINCIPAL BARKLEY RIGHT NOW!

PLEASE SEND ME TO PRISON, PRINCIPAL BARKLEY!

SO I CAN WASH THIS GROSS STUFF OFF!

OH, YOU'RE GOING SOMEPLACE WORSE THAN PRISON!
DETENTION!
TAKE HIM AWAY!

GREAT JOB, ALL OF YOU!

WELL, PUP INVESTIGATORS, YOU MAKE QUITE A P.I. PACK!
WHAT SHALL I CALL YOU?

HMMM...
"P.I. PACK." I LIKE THE SOUND OF THAT!

WHAT DO YOU THINK?

P.I. PACK IT IS!
SOUNDS GOOD TO ME!
LET'S CELEBRATE WITH SOME LUNCH!

WELL THAT SOLVES IT! AS LONG AS PAWSTON ELEMENTARY SCHOOL NEEDS PROTECTION, THE P.I. PACK IS ON THE CASE!

A NEW CASE AWAITS IN THE NEXT INSTALLMENT OF

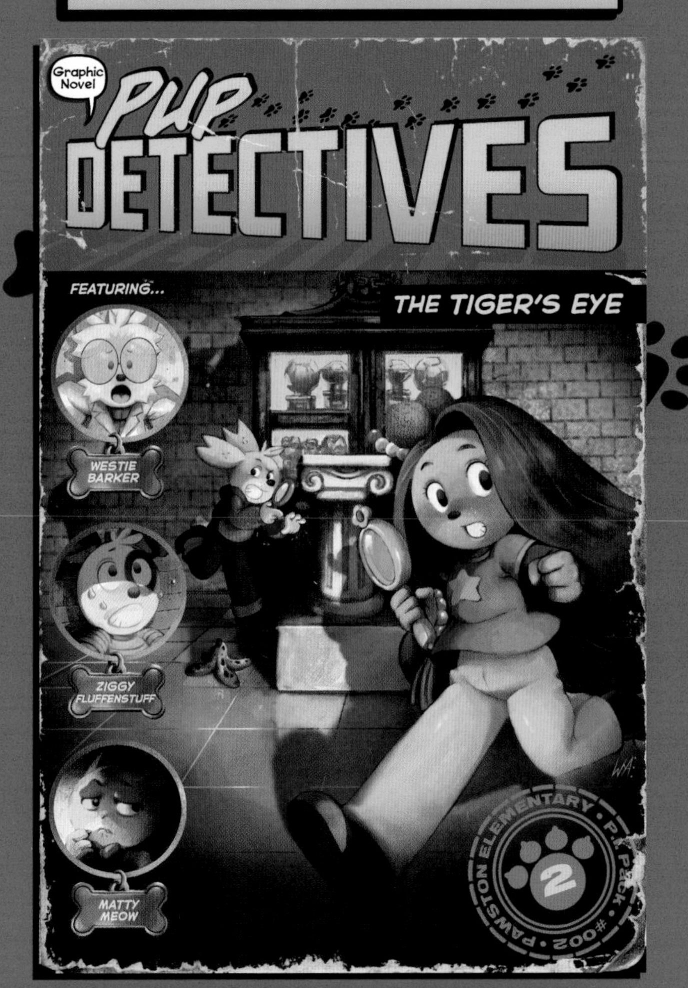

TURN THE PAGE FOR A SNEAK PEEK...

ATTENTION, PAWSTON ELEMENTARY!
BEEEEP!
THIS IS YOUR PRINCIPAL.
JUST WANTED TO REMIND YOU THAT EVERYTHING IS NORMAL AND NOTHING IMPORTANT HAS BEEN STOLEN.
OH, ALSO...
COULD THE P.I. PACK PLEASE REPORT TO MY OFFICE RIGHT AWAY?

LOOKS LIKE WE'RE ON THE CASE!